I can't let them get away, Rosie decided.

It's all their fault that Oakwood won't get any new library books this year. And they'll keep wrecking more schools until they're stopped.

She dashed away from the building, toward the car.

Just as the car pulled away from the curb, Rosie got close enough to see the number. She stopped running and wrote the license number in her notebook.

The driver of the car glanced in the rearview mirror. He saw Rosie writing in a notebook, and he hit the brakes. "That girl," he said, "is taking our license number."

The car jerked to a stop and the three men jumped out.

Rosie spun around and ran.

"Get her!" yelled one of the men.

Books by Peg Kehret

Cages
Horror at the Haunted House
Nightmare Mountain
Sisters, Long Ago
Terror at the Zoo
Frightmares™: Cat Burglar on the Prowl
Frightmares™: Bone Breath and the Vandals

Available from MINSTREL Books

FRIGHTMARES™

Bone Breath and the Vandals

Peg Kehret

A MINSTREL® BOOK

PUBLISHED BY POCKET BOOKS

New York   London   Toronto   Sydney   Tokyo   Singapore

This book is a work of fiction. Names, characters, places, and incidents are products of the author's imagination or are used fictitiously. Any resemblance to actual events or locales or persons, living or dead, is entirely coincidental.

A MINSTREL PAPERBACK *Original*

 A Minstrel Book published by
POCKET BOOKS, a division of Simon & Schuster Inc.
1230 Avenue of the Americas, New York, NY 10020

ISBN: 0-671-89189-8

First Minstrel Books paperback printing March 1995

10 9 8 7 6 5 4 3 2 1

FRIGHTMARES is a trademark of Simon & Schuster, Inc.

A MINSTREL BOOK and colophon are registered trademarks of Simon & Schuster Inc.

Cover art by Dan Burr

Printed in the U.S.A.

For Pam,
with thanks for all the phone reports

FRIGHTMARES™

Bone Breath and the Vandals

CARE CLUB
We Care About Animals

I. Whereas we, the undersigned, care about our animal friends, we promise to groom them, play with them, and exercise them daily. We will do this for the following animals:

> **WEBSTER** (Rosie's cat)
> **BONE BREATH** (Rosie's dog)
> **HOMER** (Kayo's cat)
> **DIAMOND** (Kayo's cat)

II. Whereas we, the undersigned, care about the well-being of *all* creatures, we promise to do whatever we can to help homeless animals.

III. Care Club will hold official meetings every Thursday afternoon or whenever else there is important business. All Care Club projects will be for the good of the animals.

Signed:

Rosie Saunders

Kayo Benton

Chapter

1

"*O*h, no!" Kayo Benton glanced at the headline of the morning newspaper her mother held. "They trashed *my* school?"

"I'm afraid so," Mrs. Benton said as she handed the paper to Kayo.

Quickly Kayo read the article.

VANDALS PAINT MURAL
AT OAKWOOD ELEMENTARY

The "Spray-Paint Vandals" struck again last night, this time at the Oakwood Elementary School. Somewhere between ten P.M. and midnight a tile mosaic created by last year's students was covered with graffiti.

1

Sidewalks near the mosaic were painted black.

Police Chief Brian Stravinski said he knows the approximate time because "I've had extra patrols watching every school in town. An officer checked Oakwood at ten o'clock and there was no problem. When he returned at twelve, the damage was done."

A company specializing in paint removal estimates it will cost nine thousand dollars to get all the paint off. School board members say the money spent on cleanup means Oakwood Elementary will not get any new library books this year, and the bleachers for the baseball field, scheduled for construction next month, have been postponed.

The vandals apparently did not know about a second Oakwood mural, on the back side of the building; it escaped damage.

This is the fifth vandalized school in the county this month. Despite public outrage and increased police patrols, there are no clues to the identity or motive of the vandals.

"It makes me sick," Kayo said as she gave the paper back to her mother.

Forty minutes later Kayo and her best friend, Rosie Saunders, stood on the black sidewalk, surveying the damage.

"That is the worst, meanest, most senseless thing I've ever seen in my life," said Rosie. "All our work on that mural and the vandals ruined it in one night."

The mural, made with ceramic tiles, covered one whole outside wall of Oakwood School between the door to the office and the door to the library. Last year each Oakwood student had made one tile. First, they drew a picture and then painted it on a ceramic tile. After the tiles were glazed and fired, they were permanently attached to the school wall.

In the center of the mural, cherry-red tiles without pictures spelled OAKWOOD.

Now the bright colors and happy designs were smothered with dirty words and gang symbols, all in black.

Kayo put her hand on the tile she had made. It was barely visible under the black paint. "This tile is the best artwork I ever did," she said. "Correction. This tile *was* the best artwork I ever did. It's totally ruined."

"Remember how excited we were when our tiles got added to the mural?" Rosie said. "And the special ceremony when the whole mural was done?"

Kayo nodded, blinking back tears. The mayor had come and congratulated the students on their fine work. The high school band played, and the *Daily Herald* printed a colored picture of the mural on the front page. Kayo had glued the picture in her scrapbook.

"Well, well!" said a cheerful voice behind them. "The school mural has a new look."

Turning, the girls saw Sammy Hulenback.

"Quite an improvement," said Sammy.

"Strike one," said Kayo.

"Improvement!" said Rosie. "That is the most idiotic thing you have ever said, and you say a lot of idiotic things."

"You don't like it?" said Sammy.

"The mural is ruined," said Kayo. "Don't you have any school pride?" She took off her New York Yankees cap, turned it around, and jammed it backward on her head, the way she always did in a baseball game when she was determined to throw strikes.

"It isn't ruined. It was boring before and now it's interesting."

"Strike two," said Kayo.

4

"It's going to cost the school nine thousand dollars to clean the paint off," said Rosie.

"I say leave it like it is," said Sammy. "You girls are babies if you're upset by this."

"Let's go," said Kayo. "If I stay here, I'll slug him."

As the girls marched into the school, Rosie said, "He's probably the one who did it. What a wallydraigle." She took the notebook and pencil out of her back pocket and made a check mark beside *wallydraigle*, to show she had used her vocabulary word once in ordinary conversation.

"Wallydraigle?" Kayo waited for a definition, knowing it would come.

Rosie replaced the notebook. "Wallydraigle," she said. "A feeble, imperfectly developed, or slovenly creature."

"That's Sammy, all right," Kayo said. "Feeble brain, imperfectly developed morals, and—what was the third part?"

"Slovenly. You know, untidy. Messy."

"Yep," said Kayo. "That's definitely Sammy. Sammy the wallydraigle."

"Hey, Rosie, wait up," called Sammy. "I have to ask you something."

"Now what?" said Rosie.

"Privately," said Sammy. He looked at Kayo,

clearly wanting her to leave him alone with Rosie.

"Gladly," said Kayo, and she walked away.

A few minutes later Rosie joined Kayo in their sixth-grade classroom. "You'll never believe what the wallydraigle wanted," Rosie said, making a check mark in her notebook. "He asked how you liked that poem he wrote you."

"What poem?" said Kayo. "I have completely erased any poem of his from my memory."

"He wondered what you did with it. He was hoping you sleep with it under your pillow."

"Oh, please," said Kayo. "I would have nightmares. What did he say when you told him I tore it up and threw it away?"

"I didn't say that, exactly. I didn't want to make him mad."

Kayo gave Rosie a suspicious look. "What did you say? Exactly?"

"I told him I didn't know where it was."

"It is in the wastebasket," said Kayo, "in tiny pieces. It will go from there to the recycling center."

"He said to tell you he's working on another one."

Kayo groaned.

6

"You could collect them and publish a book: *Love Poems from a Wallydraigle.*"

"Not funny."

"I'm sorry. But he doesn't listen when I tell him not to bother you. He likes you so much, he just plows on with whatever it is he plans to do, no matter what I say."

The morning announcements began. Mrs. Cushman, their sixth-grade teacher, said, "I know all of you are as angry as I am about what happened to our mural last night."

Kayo and Rosie glared at Sammy.

"Unfortunately," Mrs. Cushman went on, "the morning newspaper mentioned our school's other mural, and the police fear the vandals will take that as a challenge to come back. The police will guard our school carefully, but I urge you not to play on the school grounds after school hours for the next few weeks. Anyone who ruins public property for no reason is capable of other unreasonable and possibly violent behavior."

A shiver of apprehension rippled down Kayo's back. She glanced at Rosie, who gazed back at her with wide eyes. Clearly, Mrs. Cushman was afraid the vandals would return to Oakwood Elementary and wreck the other mural.

"The vandals have already cost us our baseball

bleachers and our new books," Mrs. Cushman said. "We do not want them to do any more damage. Above all, we want our students to be safe."

"My mom was really looking forward to bleachers," Kayo said, "so she could sit down to watch my games."

"It gives me the creeps to think of those awful people sneaking around our school with their cans of spray paint," Rosie said.

"If I ever catch them painting our other mural, I'll whop them with my bat," Kayo said.

"Ha!" said Sammy. "No way will you ever catch the vandals."

"I certainly hope not," said Mrs. Cushman.

Chapter 2

Rosie and Kayo looked nervously behind them. Even though it was daylight as they walked home from school, and the vandals always struck at night, they felt uneasy.

"I wasn't jumpy when other schools got vandalized," Kayo said, "but it's different when it's *our* school."

"I'm not in the mood for our Care Club meeting," said Rosie.

"Me, either," said Kayo.

"Let's go over to my house and take Bone Breath outside to play," said Rosie. "That would be good enough for Care Club this week."

Bone Breath greeted the girls enthusiastically, wagging and jumping and licking their hands.

"Down, Bone Breath," said Rosie.

The cairn terrier jumped some more.

"Let's play catch," Kayo suggested. "I brought my mitt."

"Bone Breath gets frustrated when we play catch; he always wants the ball. And Care Club meetings are supposed to be fun for the animals."

"Then let's play hide-and-seek. Bone Breath can run around in the trees while we play."

Rosie's house sat on two acres of land, with lots of trees and clumps of bushes. It was a great place for hide-and-seek, and, since the property was fenced, it was a safe place for Bone Breath.

While Kayo closed her eyes and counted to fifty, Rosie ran toward a clump of birch trees. Bone Breath galloped after her. "Sit," Rosie said. "Stay." Bone Breath trotted beside her. Rosie crouched behind the birch tree with the biggest trunk.

"Ready or not, here I come!" yelled Kayo.

Rosie felt hot air on the back of her neck and smelled a familiar stench. "Go away, Bone Breath," she whispered. "Go find Kayo!" Bone Breath put his head closer to hers and panted harder.

"I spy!" cried Kayo.

10

"That wasn't fair," Rosie said. "Bone Breath gave me away."

"Bone Breath must be part pointer," Kayo said.

"I told him to stay," Rosie grumbled. "He never minds."

"Why don't you take him to doggie school? My uncle took his dog and he learned to sit and stay and heel and stay off the furniture. Uncle Dan says Beano loved going to dog school and the practice sessions at home were fun."

"Bone Breath could use some manners, that's for sure," Rosie said.

"It can be an official Care Club project," Kayo said. "I'll go along to the classes, and I'll help you train Bone Breath after school every day."

"Maybe I should just take Bone Breath by myself," Rosie said. "Remember our last Care Club project, when the cat burglar locked us up?"

"That wouldn't happen again in a million years," Kayo replied. "I'll call Uncle Dan and ask where he took Beano, and then we can call them and find out about the dog obedience classes."

Five minutes later the girls sat in Rosie's kitchen while Kayo made the calls. "Talk about luck!" she said as she hung up. "A doggie kindergarten class starts tomorrow night, and they have room for Bone Breath. The only bad part is, it

11

costs thirty-five dollars and Care Club is broke, as usual. It would take a major miracle to come up with thirty-five dollars by tomorrow night."

"I'll ask my parents," Rosie said. "They might pay for it." The girls went downstairs to the studio where Rosie's father created his cartoon strips. His sign—DO NOT DISTURB OR I WILL STICK PINS UNDER YOUR TOENAILS—was not hanging on the door, so Rosie knocked.

"Would it be okay if I take Bone Breath to an obedience class at the dog school?" she asked after Mr. Saunders opened the door.

"Please do!" he said instantly. "Maybe they can teach him not to tip over the garbage can and roll around in the garbage."

"Bone Breath loves garbage," Rosie told Kayo.

"The class costs thirty-five dollars," Kayo said.

"Sign him up," said Mr. Saunders.

Kayo was always astonished that Rosie's family did not have to worry about how to pay for things. *Her* mother would have looked at the balance in the checkbook, or asked if the dog school accepted credit cards, or said they would have to wait until next month. Of course, Rosie had two parents, both of whom worked, while Kayo and her mother were on their own.

Back upstairs, Kayo said, "Think how much

fun Bone Breath will have, meeting the other dogs and having us work with him. He'll love it! And he'll learn to mind, too. I move that Care Club enroll Bone Breath in doggie school."

"I second the motion."

Kayo said, "All in favor, say aye."

"Aye," said Rosie.

"Aye," said Kayo. "Opposed?"

"Woof!" said Bone Breath.

"The motion is carried," said Kayo. "Dog school will make a big difference in Bone Breath's life. And it will be fun for us, too."

"This time," said Rosie, "I hope our Care Club project turns out the way we expect."

"It will," Kayo said. "What could go wrong at puppy kindergarten?"

Chapter 3

SPRAY-PAINT VANDALS
ATTACK CITIZEN

The Spray-Paint Vandals turned on an elderly man late last night when the man, who was walking his dog on the grounds of Discovery School, rounded the corner of the school and found three men spraying paint on the school sign. Before the man and his dog could run away, the vandals sprayed them with green paint. The man, who asked that he not be identified, is in Western Hospital, being treated for shock. He was unable to describe his attackers. The dog, who got paint in his eyes, is in Critter Care Veterinary Hospital. Dr. Adam Hastings, veterinarian, said the small white poodle may lose the sight in one eye.

Police Chief Brian Stravinski, clearly frustrated by his department's inability to catch the vandals, said, "We can't be everywhere at once. We added extra patrols last night at Oakwood, and the vandals went to Discovery instead."

The Spray-Paint Vandals have caused a total of nearly $50,000 damage, which they will be charged with when they are caught. Because of last night's incident, they are now wanted for assault, as well as for malicious mischief.

Mr. Saunders drove Rosie, Kayo, and Bone Breath to the first dog obedience class. Rosie sat in front with her father, which left Kayo in the back seat with Bone Breath, who panted harder than usual from the excitement of riding in the car. Kayo turned her head away, trying not to inhale.

Mr. Saunders helped them register and paid the fee. "I'll be back at eight-thirty," he said, "to drive you home."

A table at the side of the room contained a large coffeepot, a plate of cookies, and a box of dog biscuits. "Please help yourselves to some refreshments," said the registrar.

The girls each ate a cookie. Rosie gave a dog biscuit to Bone Breath, who swallowed it whole.

"Doesn't he ever chew?" said Kayo. "No wonder he has bad breath."

Bone Breath burped.

The other "students" were a cocker spaniel, a pair of miniature schnauzers, a giant poodle, a chihuahua, and a golden retriever. Bone Breath went wild when he saw them. He acted particularly interested in the chihuahua, which tucked its tail between its legs and quivered whenever Bone Breath got close. This only encouraged Bone Breath. He strained at the leash, panting eagerly as he tried to get closer to the chihuahua. The chihuahua's owner glared at Rosie and Kayo and carried her dog to the other side of the room.

"I hope Bone Breath is a quick learner," Kayo muttered.

"Oh, no," said Rosie. "Say it isn't true."

"What's wrong?"

"The wallydraigle just came in."

Kayo groaned.

Sammy Hulenback stood at the registration table with a humongous Saint Bernard.

"Six weeks of lessons with Sammy," Kayo said. "I'm not sure I can stand it."

"You can't desert me just because there's a wallydraigle in the class," Rosie said. "This is an official Care Club project; we're supposed to be determined. Besides, my dad already paid the fee."

"I won't desert you. But I'm staying on the opposite side of the room from Sammy."

The obedience lessons did not go the way Kayo and Rosie hoped they would. Bone Breath was far too excited to pay attention. When Rosie said "Sit" and pushed on Bone Breath's back, Bone Breath flopped on the floor and rolled over.

When the owners were told to walk the dogs in a circle, holding the leash so the dog was in the "heel" position, Bone Breath lunged and barked, trying to get to the chihuahua.

A few of the other dogs made mistakes, too, but Bone Breath was the worst.

Sammy's dog, Napoleon, behaved perfectly. Each time Bone Breath did something wrong, Sammy made snide comments.

"We'll take a ten-minute break," the instructor announced. "People potties are down the hall; doggie potty is outside." She laughed at her own humor.

Kayo and Rosie rolled their eyes at each other and rushed for the door.

"Hurry," Kayo said. "Let's go around the side of the building where Sammy won't see us."

Minutes later Sammy and his Saint Bernard rounded the corner of the building and headed straight for Rosie and Kayo. "I think there's something wrong with your dog's brain," Sammy said.

"Strike one," said Kayo.

"He's just distracted," Rosie said. "He's never been around other dogs before." She patted Bone Breath's head. Bone Breath licked her hand.

"Sit, Napoleon," Sammy said.

The Saint Bernard sat.

"Why are you here, if he already minds?" Rosie said.

"He's a fast learner," Sammy said. "Unlike a certain other dog I know." He looked at Bone Breath.

Bone Breath wagged his tail at Sammy.

"Bone Breath will learn," Rosie said.

Bone Breath tugged at the leash, trying to get closer to Napoleon. "Stop it, Bone Breath," Rosie said. Bone Breath pulled harder.

"You'll probably have the first dog ever to flunk out of doggie kindergarten," Sammy said.

"I will not!"

"Like owner, like dog."

"What's that supposed to mean?"

"Didn't you know that dogs and owners resemble each other? That's why Napoleon is handsome and smart and well behaved while that mongrel of yours is ugly and feebleminded and wouldn't know how to sit if you put a chair under him."

Rosie stomped her foot. "Leave us alone, you wallydraigle!" she shouted.

Bone Breath, sensing Rosie's anger, lunged at Sammy and tried to bite him in the ankle. The sudden movement jerked the leash out of Rosie's hand.

"Hey!" yelled Sammy. He jumped sideways, avoiding Bone Breath's teeth.

Napoleon leaped to his feet, growling and snarling at Bone Breath. Bone Breath took one look at Napoleon's size and fury, turned, and ran.

"Bone Breath!" cried Rosie. "Come back here." Bone Breath streaked across the parking lot. Rosie and Kayo raced after him.

"I ought to sic Napoleon on both of you!" Sammy yelled after them, but instead he and Napoleon returned to finish the class.

Bone Breath headed down the sidewalk, with the leash trailing behind him like the tail of a kite. Although Rosie and Kayo ran for all they were worth, the distance between them and Bone Breath increased.

As they approached the end of the block, Rosie saw cars driving down the cross street ahead. She saw a traffic light. "Bone Breath!" she yelled. "Here, Bone Breath!"

Bone Breath had never run loose before, except inside Rosie's fenced yard. He did not know to stop at a corner and look for traffic before he went into the street. And he certainly didn't know what green lights or red lights meant.

Bone Breath raced toward the corner.

"Bone Breath!" screamed Rosie. "Sit!"

Kayo, who was faster than Rosie because she ran two miles every day as part of her training to be the first female to play on a coed major league baseball team, turned on the speed. She ran so fast her Minnesota Twins cap blew off her head, but she was not as fast as Bone Breath.

As Bone Breath neared the corner, Rosie saw a car approaching from the right. "Bone Breath!" she shouted. "Come back!"

Bone Breath plunged straight ahead into the street just as the light changed to red.

Kayo yelled, "Bone Breath! Stop!"

A horn honked. Brakes squealed.

Rosie was afraid to look. Her feet pounded on the sidewalk; her heart pounded in her chest.

When Rosie reached the corner, Kayo stood on the curb waiting for her. The light was still red. A car was stopped in the middle of the intersection.

Rosie forced herself to look down at the street, in front of the car. It was empty.

The driver of the car shook his fist at Bone Breath, who was on the other side of the street, still running.

"That was close," Kayo said. She went back to retrieve her hat.

Rosie waited for the light to change. She was doubled over, with a stitch in her side. Sweat trickled down the back of her neck.

"We've lost him," Kayo said when she returned with her Twins hat. "I never saw a dog run so fast. Maybe Bone Breath is part greyhound."

"He's scared," Rosie said. "Napoleon attacked him and he's lost and now he almost got hit by a car. He probably won't stop running until he drops from exhaustion."

"What do you want to do?" Kayo said. "Should we go back to doggie kindergarten and call your dad?"

"Let's run after Bone Breath awhile longer," Rosie said. "Maybe he will get distracted by a good-smelling garbage can or another dog, and we'll catch up to him. Or maybe he'll chase a squirrel up a tree and then sit at the base of the tree and wait for it to come down, like he does at home."

The girls jogged on, although Bone Breath was no longer in sight.

In a few blocks they saw George Washington Junior High School ahead.

"Maybe he'll go to the school," Rosie said. "Sometimes my dad takes him over there and runs around the track with Bone Breath on a leash. Bone Breath might remember that, or recognize the scent."

The girls headed toward the junior high school. Just before they crossed the street to get to the school, they saw three figures huddled around the statue of George Washington that stood in the school's front yard.

"Let's ask those people if they saw Bone Breath," Rosie said, but Kayo stopped running and put her hand on Rosie's arm to restrain her.

"Shhh," Kayo said. "What are they doing?"

The girls stood still in the darkness, watching and listening.

The three figures stepped back from the statue. One of them said, "One, two, three!" and then all three raised their hands and began squirting something on the statue.

"They're spray painting George Washington," Rosie whispered.

Kayo said, "It's the vandals!"

Chapter

4

An old car was parked across the street from George Washington Junior High School. Quickly the girls knelt behind the car, peering out from behind the front tire.

"George is embarrassed," one of the men said. "He's all red in the face." The other two laughed loudly.

"You'd think they would try to be quiet," whispered Kayo. "They must know the police are looking for them."

"They're probably drunk, or on drugs."

Kayo and Rosie heard the faint hissing sound of the paint as the men squirted it on the statue.

"We have to get out of here," Kayo said. "We need to call the police."

Just then one of the men threw his can of spray paint on the ground and walked toward the car that Rosie and Kayo crouched behind.

"Stay down," Rosie whispered.

"What if he sees us?"

The girls huddled together behind the car.

Why was he coming toward them? Kayo wondered. Had he already seen them or heard them whispering?

Kayo put her head down to the ground and looked under the car. She saw the man step off the curb and start across the street. As he came closer, she could see only his tennis shoes, splattered with red paint. The shoes headed directly toward the car.

Kayo nudged Rosie and pointed, hoping Rosie would know that she meant, "He's almost here. Be ready to run if he sees us."

Rosie licked her lips and waited, barely breathing. What if the man saw them? What would he do?

When the man reached the car, he opened the door on the street side, opposite where the girls crouched. They listened, unmoving.

Seconds later the door slammed shut. Kayo peeked under the car again and saw the man's shoes walk away from the car, back across the street, toward the statue. When the girls dared to look around the tire again, they saw that the man now carried a coil of rope.

He stopped before the statue, made a loop, and lassoed the statue. The men whistled and clapped. Then they lined up, with the rope across their shoulders, and pulled.

"They're trying to tip the statue over," Rosie said.

"Let's go call the police," Kayo said. "If we hurry, they might be able to get here and catch them in the act."

"Go where? We can't knock on a stranger's door and ask to use the telephone. We might pick a house where there's someone even worse than the vandals."

"We'll have to run back to doggie school and use the phone there."

The girls peeked around the fender of the car, to be sure the men were not looking in their direction. A sudden movement on the ground near the corner of the school caught Rosie's eye. She clutched Kayo's arm.

"I saw something move," Rosie said. "I think it might be Bone Breath."

"You can't go after him now. Not here."

"We're at least six blocks from doggie kinder-

25

garten. If I go all the way back there, I'll never catch Bone Breath, and if I don't find him, he'll get hit by a car or get chewed up by a big dog like Napoleon or run and run until he drops dead from exhaustion or . . ."

Kayo held up a hand to shush Rosie. "We have to call the police," she said.

"You go call the police," Rosie said. "I'm going after Bone Breath."

"What if the vandals see you?"

"They won't. I'll go around in back of the school, by the track." Rosie didn't want to stay there alone, but Bone Breath had been her dog since she was four years old; she loved him too much not to go after him. Especially when she knew how scared he was.

Kayo knew she couldn't waste more time arguing. "If you catch him," she said, "take him back to doggie school. If you don't find him . . ." Kayo stopped, seeing the tears in Rosie's eyes. She put a hand on Rosie's arm. "You'll find him," she said. "But be careful. Don't let those vandals see you."

"I won't."

They backed away from the car. The men faced the other direction now, with the rope pulled taut across their shoulders, trying to make the statue fall that way.

"Let's go," Rosie whispered.

Kayo ran back the way they had come, looking over her shoulder several times in the first block, to be sure Rosie was okay. She didn't like leaving Rosie alone at the school, not with those hoodlums on the loose.

Rosie hurried down the sidewalk, staying on the far side of the street that ran along the side of the school. She kept a watchful eye on the backs of the three men, who were still tugging on the rope, trying to topple the statue. What jerks, she thought. She hoped Kayo's phone call would be in time.

As soon as Rosie was far enough that the school blocked her view of the men, she began to run. When she got to the corner, she started across the street, toward the back side of the school. She planned to cut across the playground to the track where her dad ran.

Just as she stepped off the curb into the street, she heard a dog bark.

Bone Breath?

The bark did not come from the track; it came from the front of the school.

Rosie stopped, listening.

The dog barked again. This time Rosie knew it was Bone Breath; he was in front of the school, where the vandals were. What if the vandals sprayed paint in Bone Breath's eyes, the way they did that other dog? He could be blinded.

She raced along the side of the school. At the corner of the building she stopped running and stayed close to the wall, moving silently around to the front side. She looked toward the statue and saw Bone Breath, less than ten feet from the three men. His tail was up and he made excited little jumps when he barked, the way he did when he saw a squirrel.

The vandals dropped the rope. One of them said, "Get out of here, dog. Scram! Beat it!" He kicked his foot in Bone Breath's direction. Bone Breath growled.

Rosie knew the men had not yet seen her. She could still slip back around the corner and run away. She hesitated. If she called Bone Breath, there was no guarantee that he would come, and the vandals would surely hear her.

Bone Breath barked again.

One of the vandals said, "Stupid dog. You asked for it." The three men grabbed their cans of spray paint and aimed them at Bone Breath's face.

"Here, Bone Breath," called Rosie, clapping her hands together. "Come, Bone Breath!"

Together, the three vandals turned toward her, like puppets on the same string. For a long instant they froze, staring at Rosie.

Rosie motioned to Bone Breath. "Come!" she called.

Bone Breath barked again.

"Bone Breath!" Rosie shouted. "Come!"

The vandals sprang into action. One of them threw his can of spray paint at Bone Breath, hitting him in the side. Bone Breath yelped and took off, galloping away from Rosie and around the other side of George Washington Junior High.

Rosie spun around and dashed back along the side of the school, the way she had just come. Fear made her legs move faster than she had ever run before. What if the men came after her? Where could she hide?

When she reached the back corner of the school, she looked over her shoulder.

The three men were running across the street toward the old car that Rosie and Kayo had knelt behind. Rosie took a deep breath and blew it out. Flattening herself against the building, she watched the men climb into the car.

29

They're going to get away, Rosie thought. The police haven't come and the vandals are going to get away again and they won't be caught because I can't give a good description of the car.

She couldn't identify the men, either. In the brief moment when they saw her, she had focused her attention on Bone Breath. She had an overall impression of three mean-looking men, but she had no specific details that would help the police locate them.

The car doors slammed shut.

She wrinkled her nose, holding her glasses in place, and tried to see the car better. Rosie didn't know enough about cars to say what make the car was and, even with the streetlight, it was hard to be certain if the color was black or blue or maybe a dark maroon. All she knew for sure was that it was old and full of dents. Why hadn't she paid more attention when she was close to it?

I should have taken down their license plate number, Rosie realized. As soon as the man took the rope out of that car, we knew the car belonged to the vandals, and it would have been easy to write the license plate number in my vocabulary notebook when Kayo and I were standing right next to the car. Why didn't I think of that?

The engine started.

Rosie stood next to the school building, torn between chasing after Bone Breath before he got too far ahead of her, and trying to see the vandals' license plate number.

I'm so close, she thought. If the men drive away now, it could be weeks before they're caught. Other kids might lose their library books and their baseball bleachers. The vandals might *never* be captured.

I can't let them get away, Rosie decided. It's all their fault that Oakwood won't get any new library books this year. And they'll keep wrecking more schools until they're stopped.

She dashed away from the building, toward the car.

As Rosie ran toward the street, she reached in her pocket for her vocabulary notebook and pencil. Just as the car pulled away from the curb, Rosie got close enough to see the license plate. She stopped running and wrote the number in her notebook.

The driver of the car glanced in the rearview mirror. He saw Rosie writing in a notebook, and he hit the brakes. "That girl," he said, "is taking our license plate number."

"The little creep," said one of the others.

The car jerked to a stop and the three men jumped out, leaving the car in the middle of the street.

Rosie spun around and ran.

"Get her!" yelled one of the men.

Chapter

5

Rosie urged her legs to run faster, but they were already going at top speed.

The footsteps of the vandals thudded on the ground behind her.

Rosie reached the back of the school and started across the playground, her feet hitting the asphalt so hard that sharp slivers of pain went up the backs of her legs.

I should have been more careful, she thought. I should never have let them see me writing down their license plate number. What if they catch me? What will they do? She could deny that she was writing down their number, but if they searched her, the evidence was right there in her hand.

As she ran, she opened the notebook. She tore out the last page, where she had written the license number, and crumpled it in her fist.

When she passed the garbage Dumpster at the back of the school, she tossed the paper toward it. It was not unusual for a stray piece of paper to blow free when someone dumped trash. In the dark the men chasing her probably would not see it, and even if they did, they would pay no attention. She jammed the notebook back in her pocket and ran on, headed for the track.

She left the asphalt and ran through the grass that bordered the track. Just before she reached the track, a hand pressed down on her shoulder, forcing her to stop.

Panting, Rosie turned to look at the three men. The yard light from the playground area allowed her to see their faces. The one with his hand on her shoulder was tall and skinny, with pockmarks on his face. The one who had come after the rope was stocky, with a bushy beard. The third man was average height and weight and would have looked like an ordinary person except he had a gold ring in his nose. All three wore jackets with a strange red and purple insignia on them. Gang members, Rosie thought.

"Let me go," Rosie said.

"No way," said Ring Nose. "You were watching us."

"I wasn't. My dog ran away and I heard him bark and I was trying to catch him."

"She saw us," said Bushy Beard. "She knows."

"I don't know what you're talking about," Rosie said. "I was chasing my dog and I heard him bark and when I looked for him, you were there."

"She saw us," repeated Bushy Beard. "She knows what we were doing, and now she knows what we look like."

"I didn't see you do anything," Rosie said.

"No?" said Tall Man. "You didn't see anything, but you decided, for no reason at all, to run after my car and write down my license plate number."

"I didn't write down any license plate number. I have a vocabulary notebook and I wrote down a vocabulary word. Wallydraigle."

"Sure you did," said Ring Nose. "Funny that you had to run after our car in order to do it."

Rosie held out her notebook. "Look for yourselves, if you don't believe me," she said.

The tall man let go of Rosie and took the notebook, but instead of opening it, he threw it on the ground. "We don't need to look at anything," he said. "We know you saw us and you were planning to turn us in."

"That was not a smart move," said Ring Nose.

"Not smart," repeated Bushy Beard.

"You were going to tell the cops about us," said the tall man, "and we don't like finks, do we, men?"

Rosie eyed the three men. Their faces were flushed, their eyes had a wild, glazed look, and she could smell liquor on their breath. *Hurry, Kayo,* she thought. *Get the police here quickly.*

"What should we do with her?" said Bushy Beard.

"Let's tie her to George Washington and paint her red," said Ring Nose.

"She can be Martha Washington," said the tall one.

The other two laughed as if that were the funniest joke they'd ever heard.

"Let's go, Martha," the tall one said as he shoved Rosie from behind. "Georgy-porgy is waiting for you."

All three men roared with laughter as Rosie stumbled forward.

Bushy Beard grabbed one of Rosie's arms, and Ring Nose grabbed the other. With the tall man behind them, they escorted Rosie toward the front of the school, where the statue was.

Rosie did not struggle. What good would it do?

Stall them, she told herself. Stall them until the police get here.

"My friend will be back any minute," Rosie said. "She went to call . . ." She started to say "to call the police," but realized if she said that, the vandals would know she had lied when she said she had not seen what they were doing. "To call my dad," Rosie finished. "About my dog."

"Someone else saw us?" said Ring Nose.

"She saw my dog. I told you, we were looking for my dog."

Bushy Beard stopped. "We can't tie her to the statue and paint her," he said. "Not if her friend is on the way back. She'll be found too soon; we won't have time to get far enough away."

"She knows what we look like," said Ring Nose.

They let go of Rosie and looked at the tall man.

"We'll take her with us," he said.

"Right," said Bushy Beard. "Take her for a little ride."

Rosie swallowed. She shouldn't have said anything about Kayo. It would be better to be tied to the statue and painted red than to be taken prisoner by the men.

She looked around. The school yard was empty. Why didn't the police come? Had something happened to Kayo?

Behind her, the tall man stepped closer. She could sense his presence behind her, could hear him breathing hard. The other two stayed in front of her, their cold eyes looking Rosie up and down.

"Let's go," said Ring Nose. "I say we take her out in the country and teach her a lesson."

Bushy Beard moved closer to Rosie. "Teach her not to sneak around, spying on people," he said.

"And not to tattle," said Ring Nose.

The three men surrounded her, their dark eyes hinting at their evil intentions.

Rosie screamed, a shrill, loud scream that made her tonsils hurt.

Ring Nose clamped his hand over her mouth, jerking her head back sharply and holding it there.

The scream stopped.

Chapter

6

Kayo sprinted all the way back to dog school, running the way she would if she was on third base and the batter had just hit a single to left. She burst in the door as the trainer told the dogs to sit.

"Where's the phone?" Kayo gasped. "I have to call the police."

Startled dogs barked at the interruption.

"What happened?" asked the instructor. "Where is your friend? Where is her dog?"

"Bone Breath probably attacked someone," said Sammy. "He's vicious, you know. He attacked Napoleon during the break."

"Oh, my," said the owner of the chihuahua.

All the other dog owners began talking at once.

Quickly the instructor showed Kayo the telephone. Kayo called 911. "I saw the school vandals," Kayo said. "They're at George Washington Junior High right now, painting the statue in the school yard."

The operator who took the call relayed the information via computer and then asked Kayo's name and address.

"Kathryn Elizabeth Benton," she said. Ever since she hurled a no-hitter in the baseball playoffs, the first pitcher in the Oakwood School District to do so, everyone except her mother had called her Kayo, but she thought she should give the police her full legal name.

When she finished talking to the emergency operator, she tried to call Rosie's parents, to tell them that Bone Breath had run off. She got the Saunderses' answering machine. Kayo hung up without leaving a message. Mr. Saunders would be back at dog school before he got a message.

"So where is Rosie now?" asked Sammy.

"Still looking for Bone Breath. Or, if she's found him, she is on the way back here."

Kayo looked at the clock on the wall; it was eight o'clock. Mr. Saunders had said he would pick them up when dog school ended at eight-thirty, so she sat down to wait for Rosie or Mr. Saunders, whoever arrived first.

The instructor tried to get the class going again, but the owners and the dogs were too excited by the interruption and none of them could settle down. Even Napoleon, the star pupil, refused to sit when Sammy told him to.

"We'll take her to the fishing hole," the tall one said. "That will be deserted at night."

"Gag her first," said Bushy Beard, "or someone might hear her while we're getting her in the car. We don't need any do-gooder citizen calling the cops."

Ring Nose removed a dirty red bandanna from his pocket. When the tall man took his hand off Rosie's mouth, Ring Nose stuffed the bandanna in, pushing it back so that Rosie could not make a sound. The bandanna tasted and smelled like paint.

The tall man held her arms behind her back until the bandanna was in place.

Meanwhile, Bushy Beard retrieved the rope which they had left dangling on the statue of George Washington.

Rosie did not try to get away. There were three

of them, and they were all bigger than she. Any fight could only end with her being injured.

Even if she managed to slip out of their grasp, they were faster than she was—they had already proved that—and would only catch her again. Her best hope was to cooperate and stall for time and hope that Kayo had called the police by now and that they would arrive soon.

Moving quickly, the men tied Rosie's hands behind her back and wound the rope around her ankles so she could not walk.

"She's small enough to fit in the trunk," the tall man said.

The trunk! Rosie wondered if she should have struggled, after all. She imagined herself shut in the trunk of a car, being driven to a lonely country lane, and then—and then what? She would not allow herself to imagine what could happen next.

"We'll have to carry her to the car," Ring Nose said.

"No problem," said the tall man. He picked Rosie up and flung her over his shoulder. Carrying Rosie like a sack of potatoes, he strode toward the car with Bushy Beard and Ring Nose beside him.

As they reached the front of the school, a low

growl came from the shadows next to the building.

"Here comes that pesky dog again," said Bushy Beard.

Silently Rosie pleaded, *Go away, Bone Breath. They'll only hurt you if you try to help me. Go away.*

Bone Breath barked.

"I'm going to fix that dog once and for all," said Ring Nose. He started toward Bone Breath.

Rosie wriggled and twisted, trying to distract the men.

"Hold still," muttered the tall man. He shifted her weight on his shoulder and tightened his grip on her legs.

With her head dangling upside down against the tall man's back, Rosie watched Ring Nose approach Bone Breath.

He'll run away, Rosie thought. Bone Breath knows one of these men threw the paint can at him. He's scared of them.

Bone Breath barked again.

"Come here, dog," said Ring Nose. "Nice dog."

Run, Bone Breath, thought Rosie. *Get away.*

Bone Breath stopped barking and watched nervously as Ring Nose approached.

*   *   *

43

Officer Ken Bremner made an extra circle around Oakwood Elementary School, aiming his patrol car's spotlight at every side of the building. It was his break time, when he would normally pull in to the parking lot of the Country Buffet and relax for ten or fifteen minutes, but tonight he was more interested in watching the schools than in getting his usual black coffee and apple pie.

All was quiet at Oakwood Elementary, so Officer Bremner drove on. He was less than a mile from the Country Buffet when the call crackled over the radio in his patrol car.

Attention all units: Vandals sighted at George Washington Junior High School. Cross streets: Tenth and Elm. Suspects are painting the statue of Washington in the school's front courtyard. Advise if you are in the area. Ten-four.

Officer Bremner responded that he was on his way, made a U-turn in the middle of the street, and stomped his foot on the accelerator. He wanted this one. He could almost taste the sweetness of catching those jokers in the act.

At the corner of Fourth and Maple, he turned on his siren. He would have preferred to approach the school silently, and not give the vandals any warning, but there were other cars on Maple

44

Drive and he had to get them safely out of his way.

As he turned down Tenth, the street George Washington Junior High was on, he heard two other cars call in, saying they were also headed for the school.

Good, Bremner thought. Good because they were far enough behind him that he was sure to get there first and have the pleasure of arresting the vandals himself. But also good because it was nice to know other cops were on the way, in case the vandals gave him trouble.

"Here, dog," said Ring Nose.

No! thought Rosie. *Don't go to him. He'll hurt you.* She tried to kick but the tall man held on tighter.

"Good dog," said Ring Nose. He knelt on one knee and extended his hand. "Good, stupid dog."

Bone Breath wagged his tail.

In her mind Rosie screamed silently: *Run, Bone Breath! Run for your life!*

A siren shrieked in the distance.

The three men froze. For a second no one moved; no one spoke.

The siren shrieked again, the shrill noise slicing through the dark night.

Ring Nose stood up, turned away from Bone Breath, and spoke to his companions. "Cops." There was loathing in his voice, and terror.

Bushy Beard said all the words that had been painted on the Oakwood mural, plus a few more.

"We have to get out of here," said Ring Nose. "Come on! Get the girl in the trunk."

Rosie's skin prickled with fear.

The tall man put Rosie down. She teetered, finding it hard to get balanced with her feet tied together, and almost fell.

"I'm not taking the girl," the tall man said. "What if the cops stop us? What if they check the car? We'd be charged with kidnapping."

"We can't leave her here," said Ring Nose. "They'll find her right away."

The siren was louder now. Closer.

Bushy Beard swore again. Rosie wondered what percentage of his vocabulary consisted of gutter words.

The siren was joined by a second siren and then a third. The trio rose and fell, like a chorus of wolves howling. *Hurry*, thought Rosie. *Hurry!*

She saw panic in the men's eyes.

"The Dumpster," said the tall man.

The other two looked around.

"We'll put her in the Dumpster," said the tall

man. "They won't find her in there until the garbage truck comes."

"And maybe not then," added Bushy Beard.

The tall man stood behind Rosie, his hands on her shoulders. Ring Nose grabbed Rosie's ankles and lifted them until she hung between the men like a hammock suspended between two trees.

Bone Breath came closer, barking at the men.

Carrying Rosie, the tall man and Ring Nose ran toward the big green Dumpster that sat at the back edge of the playground.

Bone Breath woofed furiously, circling around the men as they ran. Ring Nose kicked at him and missed.

Bushy Beard reached the Dumpster first, lifted the metal top, and held it open. When the men tried to lift her over the side, Rosie kicked and squirmed. Maybe she could stall them long enough for the police to get there. The cops would hear Bone Breath barking. They would come to the back of the school and investigate.

"Hold still," Tall Man muttered, "or you'll go in the Dumpster dead, and your flea-bitten mutt with you."

Rosie quit fighting.

Ring Nose said, "One, two, *three.*"

On the word *three* they heaved Rosie over the side of the Dumpster.

Thud! She landed in a heap of garbage.

Bone Breath quit barking. He whined and ran around the Dumpster, sniffing the ground.

"Let's put the dog in, too," Ring Nose said.

"We don't have time to fool with a dog," said the tall man. "Move it!"

Bushy Beard called down to her. "If they find you, you have no idea who put you there. You got that? No descriptions. No license plate number. No nothing. Because if you tell the cops anything at all, we'll come after you. We'll find you. And next time you'll get far worse than being dumped in the garbage. You got that?"

Rosie could not respond with the bandanna stuffed in her mouth, but Ring Nose did not wait for an answer anyway.

The metal top clanged shut.

Rosie could not hear the men anymore, but she knew what they were doing. They were running to their car. If they got there before the police arrived, they would get in and start the engine and drive away from the school as if they were ordinary people on their way home from the movies or out to do some shopping. She fervently hoped the police arrived before the men got away.

She couldn't hear Bone Breath anymore. What if he was chasing the vandals? It would be just like him to run after them and bark and nip at their heels. Hard telling what they would do to the plucky little dog if they ever caught him.

The sirens sounded faint from inside the Dumpster, and Rosie could not judge whether they were closer or not. Then, abruptly, they stopped.

Rosie was surrounded by silence.

Chapter 7

Officer Bremner turned off the siren as he approached the school, his glance darting in all directions. He saw no one. No cars. No people. Nothing.

Officer Bremner stopped his patrol car directly in front of the school, as close as he could get to the statue of George Washington without driving up over the curb and on to the grass.

He swore softly under his breath, knowing he was too late. They were gone. Once again the vandals had escaped.

He got out of the car and looked up at the bright red statue. "They really did a number on you, George, old pal," he said.

Empty cans of spray paint lay at the base of the statue, as if taunting him.

Bremner swore again at the close miss. He had hoped he might catch them this time. Catch them and arrest them and put an end to all the outcry from the press and the public. And put an end to the pressure from his boss.

Chief Stravinski was embarrassed by the inability of his people to stop the vandalism, and he was throwing a fit. Yesterday was the worst, when the *Daily Herald* hinted that a police chief who couldn't protect the city's schools must be inept and asked if it was time for a new police chief. You could have heard Stravinski yelp clear across town when he read that.

Bremner could testify that when the chief was in hot water, everyone under him got scalded, too.

But it wasn't just that Bremner wanted to save his own skin from Chief Stravinski's wrath. It went deeper than that. Much deeper. Officer Ken Bremner grew up in Oakwood. He had played football on all the school fields and gone to concerts in the school auditoriums. And now his daughter, his Jessica, the light of his life, was almost old enough to start school, and he wanted her to have the best schooling she could get in buildings that were clean and safe.

This was his town and these were his schools

that were being trashed, and Bremner did not cotton to folks messing with what was his. It would give him great personal pleasure to get his hands on whoever was responsible and see that they had plenty of time behind bars to think about changing their ways.

As two other patrol cars pulled up in front of the school, Bremner hurried around to the back side of the school, toward the playground. Maybe the vandals were still hiding somewhere on the grounds. Maybe they hadn't run away but were crouched somewhere in the shadows.

As he rounded the corner of the building, Bremner turned on his flashlight, arcing it quickly across the back of the school building.

A dog barked. Bremner shined the light in that direction. The dog was alone, standing beside the garbage Dumpster. It was a short, stocky dog with shaggy gray hair and small pointed ears. It barked again. Probably a hungry stray, Bremner thought. A stray, who could smell leftover pizza inside the Dumpster and was barking in frustration because he was unable to reach it.

He moved the light across the yard again. When he was certain the school yard was empty, Officer Bremner aimed the light back at the dog for a closer look. A shiny spot on the dog's neck reflected the light. A collar.

Officer Bremner sighed. It wasn't a stray, after all. The dog wore a collar, so why was it running loose like this? There was a leash law in Oakwood. Why didn't people take care of their animals?

"It's okay, boy," he said. "Good dog."

The dog wagged its tail tentatively and backed warily away from Officer Bremner. Something moved beside the dog. Bremner stepped closer and saw a brown leash dragging on the ground. The fool dog must have jerked away from its owner while it was out for a walk. So why wasn't the owner close by, looking for the dog?

Officer Bremner remembered the elderly man and his poodle who tangled with the vandals. Had something similar happened here? Maybe he should take the dog with him and try to contact the owner.

He went forward and reached for the leash. The dog skittered away. Officer Bremner went after him, but the dog was small and quick.

Officer Bremner went back to his patrol car, fished in the litter bag, and removed a small sack that was half full of french fries. His beeper had gone off in the middle of lunch, and by the time

Bremner took care of the problem, the fries were cold.

Carrying the french fries, Bremner returned to the Dumpster. Instead of trying to catch the dog, he knelt down and put the bag of french fries on the ground beside him, keeping a few in his hand. One at a time he threw them to the dog, who gobbled them down as quickly as he could. When Bremner quit tossing fries at him, the dog came forward, tail wagging, to eat those that were left in the bag. It was simple for Officer Bremner to reach down and grab the leash.

It was not so simple to lead the dog to the car. The animal refused to budge. After the fries were gone, the dog braced its legs on the ground and wouldn't move.

When Officer Bremner tried to pick the dog up, it growled and snapped at him. He let go. He didn't need a dog bite, and he couldn't waste any more time trying to get the dog in the car. The vandals couldn't be too far away; they might even be on their way to Oakwood Elementary, and Oakwood El was Bremner's responsibility that night.

Officer Bremner turned and walked back to his patrol car. He would have to call County Animal Control and have them come and pick the dog up. He hated to do it. Too often, dog owners didn't contact Animal Control in time to get their dog back.

Animal Control only held an animal for forty-eight hours, and some people waited longer than that to inquire, thinking the dog was lost and would find its way back home. It would be a shame, Officer Bremner thought, for a cute dog like that to be put down, even if the owners were irresponsible.

Well, he couldn't waste the night worrying about a dog. He had work to do. He returned to the front of the school, where other officers were carefully dusting the paint cans for fingerprints, and reported that the vandals were not in back of the school.

He got in his patrol car and called Animal Control as he drove away, headed for Oakwood Elementary School.

It was dark as a moonless midnight inside the Dumpster, but Rosie did not need light in order to know what she was lying on. The smell made Bone Breath's mouth seem like a fresh tube of toothpaste. It was rotten lettuce and moldy pizza and two-day-old tuna casserole, magnified a thousand times. With the lid shut, the odor had no-where to go—except into Rosie's nostrils.

In her mind she saw the cafeteria garbage cans at the end of lunch period each day—overflowing with half-eaten bologna sandwiches, banana peels, apple cores, and candy wrappers. She pic-tured the cafeteria staff scraping leftover spa-ghetti, chicken bones, and tapioca pudding into more garbage cans, all of which were eventually emptied into the Dumpster.

She was, she knew, lying on all of the above, plus half-eaten hot dogs, rejected broccoli, sour-smelling milk cartons, and coffee grounds from the teachers' lounge. Not to mention the con-tents of the bathroom wastebaskets.

Rosie's stomach lurched. You can't get sick, she told herself. There is no way you can throw up when there's a paint rag stuffed in your mouth.

She wondered how long it would take before she was found. The police should be arriving at the school any minute, but they would go to the front, by the statue. Unless they were there al-ready, Rosie knew they would be too late to catch the vandals. By now the three men were probably speeding away in their car, looking for another school to damage.

Well, the vandals were the least of her problems. She could identify them, and both she and Kayo would testify that the vandals painted the statue and tried to tip it over. If they didn't get caught tonight, they would surely be caught soon.

Not for one minute did Rosie consider obeying Bushy Beard's instructions not to tell what she knew. He could threaten all he wanted, but as soon as she got out of this Dumpster, Rosie intended to find the piece of paper that had the license plate number on it and turn it in. She would also describe all three of the men in detail. It shouldn't be too hard for the police to find them by tracing the license plate number on the car.

She wondered what time it was. When her dad arrived to take them home from doggie school, Kayo would tell him what had happened. Dad would drive Kayo over here, to see if Bone Breath was running around the track. And then—and then, what? Whether Bone Breath was here or not, they would never open the school Dumpster and look inside. Why should they?

Dad would call her name, and when she didn't answer, he would drive around the area, looking for her. Eventually he and Mom would notify the police, and the whole town would be searching, but she doubted very much if anyone would think to look for her in a Dumpster.

She would probably have to spend the night here, nestled in rotting peanut butter sandwiches. Rosie's stomach lurched again.

Thank goodness there was school tomorrow. Someone would carry trash out to the Dumpster and throw it in. What a surprise they would get when they discovered Rosie!

If they discovered Rosie. Who looks in the Dumpster before they toss in the trash? Nobody. They simply crack the lid, hoist their load, and let it fall. And when school was in session, there was always so much racket coming from the playground that no one would hear her moan.

Splat! The garbage would go all over Rosie.

By this time tomorrow she could be buried alive in garbage.

"Woof!"

Rosie, immersed in her terrible daydream, jumped at the sound.

"Woof! Woof!"

It was Bone Breath, and it sounded as if he was right next to the Dumpster.

Rosie tensed. Did that mean the vandals had come back? Is that who he was barking at?

58

Maybe they waited until the police had searched the school yard and left and then returned for Rosie.

Or maybe the police were here, searching the school yard. Maybe Bone Breath was barking at a cop.

She listened but heard no voices. She waited. No one lifted the Dumpster lid.

She groaned but the sound was so muffled by the bandanna in her mouth that she doubted anyone would hear it, even if they were standing right next to the Dumpster.

Bone Breath barked again.

A new, even worse, picture flashed into Rosie's brain. The garbage truck! She knew the county garbage truck emptied the Oakwood Elementary Dumpster. The garbage truck came in the evening, and Rosie had seen it more than once when she was there to watch Kayo's baseball team play. What if the garbage truck came here before she was discovered?

She knew exactly what happened when the garbage truck came. It always gave a loud *Beep! Beep! Beep!* as it backed up, to warn people to get out of the way.

A huge clawlike lift reached down from the back of the truck, slid under the Dumpster, gripped the bottom, and raised the Dumpster into the air like a hawk carrying away a field mouse. When the Dumpster was high enough, the lift pulled in and tilted, dumping the contents into the garbage truck's gaping mouth.

As the contents entered the truck, the grinders started. Like giant teeth, they chewed all the garbage into tiny pieces, grinding chicken bones and shredding pizza crust.

What would the garbage grinders do to a person?

Stop it! Rosie thought. It won't help to lie here getting hysterical over something that might not ever happen. Be calm and figure out how to help yourself.

Usually, when she wanted to calm herself, the first thing she did was take a deep breath. Under the circumstances, she decided to skip that step.

Chapter

Sitting on the sidelines at doggie school, Kayo was even more restless than the dogs. Each time she looked at the clock, she expected it to say 8:30. The first time she looked, it said 8:04. She asked one of the dog owners for the time, to be sure the clock was correct. It was.

The second time she looked, it said 8:09 and then, incredibly, when she looked the third time it *still* said 8:09.

She wondered where Rosie was. Had she caught Bone Breath? Were the vandals still at the school? Did they see Rosie?

I can't stand this waiting, Kayo thought. There is time for me to run back to George Washington Junior High, find Rosie, and get back here before

Mr. Saunders arrives. That would be better than sitting here doing nothing and wondering what was happening at the school. With any luck, Rosie had found Bone Breath by now and was on her way back to dog school. Kayo would meet them partway.

As the instructor explained the importance of praising your dog whenever he does something right, Kayo slipped out the door. If she ran really fast, she could get to the school in ten minutes. Maybe she would arrive while the police were still there and could watch the vandals get arrested. Then she would find Rosie and still get back to dog school before Mr. Saunders arrived to drive them home.

Kayo ran at top speed, as if she were trying to steal a base. She saw the school ahead. Two police cars were parked in front of it, their blue lights circling. Excitement gave her fresh energy.

As she ran the last block, two police officers got in the patrol cars.

Kayo stopped running. The police were alone. Where were the vandals? She watched as the police cars drove away from the school, going in two different directions. One passed her and she looked carefully to see if the vandals might be in the backseat. It was empty.

She looked toward the corner where she and Rosie had crouched behind the old car. It was gone.

Disappointment slowed her feet. Her call had been too late. The vandals got away, again.

Kayo walked the rest of the way to the school. When she reached the statue of George Washington, the school yard seemed too silent. She had expected to find an arrest in progress. Instead, she found nothing.

Kayo walked around the base of the statue. The rope that had been looped around George Washington's neck was gone. Except for the bright red paint on the statue, there was no sign that anyone had been there. No empty paint cans or other litter. No police; no vandals. Most disturbing of all, there was no Rosie.

She felt creepy standing there, knowing that only a short time earlier, the vandals had stood in that exact spot. What if they returned?

She wondered if Rosie was in back of the school, still trying to catch Bone Breath. She decided to go around the building and take a look at the track where Mr. Saunders and Bone Breath jogged, just in case Rosie was back there, chasing Bone Breath.

She hurried around the side of the building and

started across the playground. If Rosie wasn't there, she would leave. Kayo did not like prowling around alone at night this way. Her mother would have a fit if she knew where Kayo was, and Kayo had to admit her mother was right. Kayo wished she had waited for Mr. Saunders before coming back to the school.

"Woof! Woof!"

Kayo jumped at the sharp sound. Bone Breath stood in front of the school Dumpster, barking at her.

Under normal circumstances, Kayo would have called Bone Breath to come to her, but tonight she didn't want to attract any attention. What if the vandals came back? What if they were lurking in the shadows around the school, waiting for a chance to do more damage? She didn't want anyone to know she was here.

Instead of calling, she walked silently toward Bone Breath. He barked twice more and then, apparently recognizing her, quit barking and started to wag his tail.

Kayo ran to Bone Breath and petted him, relieved to see that the dog was unharmed. Bone Breath licked her hand and his tail went into high speed.

"Come on, boy," Kayo whispered, as she picked up the leash. "I'll take you home."

Kayo walked away from the Dumpster, but Bone Breath did not follow. When the leash grew taut, he sat down, planting himself firmly beside the Dumpster.

Annoyed, Kayo tugged sharply at the leash. Bone Breath stayed put. If any dog ever needed obedience class, Kayo thought, it was surely Bone Breath. After almost being hit by a car, you would think he would be glad to go home with Kayo. Instead, he stubbornly stayed next to the Dumpster.

Kayo pulled again. When Bone Breath did not respond this time, she decided to carry him. She put her arms around Bone Breath and started to lift him. Bone Breath growled. Surprised, Kayo let go.

What was wrong with him? Why wouldn't he come with her? Normally, he was a friendly, happy dog who gladly tagged after anyone who talked to him. Now he acted as if the garbage Dumpster was his home and she was trying to take him away from it.

Then Kayo remembered Rosie had said Bone Breath loved garbage. Probably he could smell what he thought were wonderful odors seeping out of the Dumpster. She tried one more time to pick him up but Bone Breath struggled and kicked so much she couldn't hang on.

Muttering under her breath, Kayo wound the handle of the leash around one leg of the Dumpster and tied a knot. At least that way, Bone Breath could not run off and get lost again. She would go back to dog school, wait for Mr. Saunders, and bring him back here. Then he could wrestle Bone Breath into the car and take him home.

Kayo headed back the way she had come. Partway across the asphalt playground, she stepped on something and her foot slipped out from under her. Kayo fell, landing on her hands and knees. When she looked to see what she had stepped on, goose bumps rose on her arms and legs.

Rosie's notebook. Even in the dim light, Kayo recognized the blue notebook that Rosie carried constantly in her pocket.

Rosie would never lose her vocabulary notebook. She took it out only to add a new word or to make a check mark beside her current word after she used it. And she was always careful to replace the notebook in her pocket. If she had dropped it, she would have picked it up. How did the notebook get here? Where was Rosie?

Kayo's mind bubbled with possibilities. What if the vandals saw Rosie? Maybe they caught her and she struggled and during the fight, her notebook fell out of her pocket. Or maybe they made Rosie go with them and she dropped the notebook on purpose, as a way to let Kayo know she was in trouble.

You're jumping to conclusions, Kayo told herself. Lots of people buy little blue notebooks. Lots of people use the school playground. You're getting all worked into a froth, and this probably doesn't even belong to Rosie.

Kayo picked up the notebook and opened it.

She tipped it toward the playground light, squinting as she flipped quickly through the pages. The words leaped from the paper like fish jumping for flies, and each one brought memories of Rosie, with her ever-present dictionary.

It was Rosie's notebook, all right. No one else in the whole world would carry around definitions for words like *ineffable* and *wallydraigle*.

Kayo tried to swallow the fear that rose in her throat. Rosie was a unique, one-of-a-kind girl, Kayo's best friend, and now something had happened to her.

Something terrible.

Chapter

*O*fficer Bremner rested his head on the back of the seat and closed his eyes. Although he had pulled his patrol car into the station's parking lot several minutes ago, he still sat in the car, thinking.

Something niggled at the back of Officer Bremner's mind. It was a vague feeling, a nagging suspicion that he had missed something. But what? He had seen the paint cans; he knew the other officers would pick them up and take them to the lab. The only other unusual thing at the school was the little dog barking at the Dumpster, and he had reported that. What else was there? Nothing. And yet the feeling persisted.

Mentally he retraced his actions at the junior

high. He could think of nothing he should have done.

He looked at his watch. His shift had ended five minutes ago, so why was he still sitting here in the dark? He should be in his own car by now, on his way home, looking forward to a bowl of granola before he climbed into bed. Yet, here he sat.

Why? Because years of experience had taught Officer Bremner to listen to his hunches. Common sense told him he had done everything he should at the school, but he couldn't shake the sense that he had overlooked something. Possibly something important.

Might as well go back and check the place again, he decided. I won't get any sleep until I do.

He backed out of his parking space and returned to George Washington Junior High.

The bright red George Washington stood guard on an empty school yard; the other officers had finished their business and departed. Sensible fellows, he thought. *They* didn't hang around after hours, putting in their own time on what was likely a wild-goose chase.

Slowly Officer Bremner retraced his earlier steps. When he got to the back of the school and shined his flashlight at the Dumpster, two bright eyes glinted in the light.

The dog was still there, sitting next to the Dumpster. Officer Bremner wasn't surprised. Even in daylight Animal Control was not noted for its prompt response, and night calls always took longer.

The dog stood up and shook itself. Bremner looked again. The leash was tied to one of the Dumpster's legs. The dog had not been tied earlier. Who had been here? Why would anyone do that?

He walked closer. The dog barked once and then sat down, as if it had barked as much as it could for one night.

A scrap of paper fluttered in the slight breeze and the dog playfully jumped at it and then stopped, sniffed the paper, and wagged its tail. Bremner smiled. It was a cute little dog, and Bremner half regretted turning it in to Animal Control. He could have taken it with him, put an ad in the newspaper, and tried to find the owner.

But if he started picking up every lost dog he came across, the chief would have his hide. He could almost hear Stravinski's rough voice: "You are not Animal Control. You're a cop with a beat, not a rescue service for runaway mutts."

The odd feeling persisted. It was a know-ingness, a sense that something important was right under his nose, if only he would pay attention. Bremner bent and patted the dog's head. The dog promptly rolled over and offered its belly to be scratched. Officer Bremner rubbed the dog's stomach, and then, before he straightened up, he picked up the scrap of paper.

He smoothed it out and held his light on it. A license plate number had been scribbled on the paper. Bremner's blood raced faster. He started back to his car.

It could be coincidence, he knew. It might have nothing to do with the vandals.

Then again, there *had* been a witness this time. The girl who called in the tip that the vandals were here did not have a license plate number, but maybe someone else had seen the men with their cans of spray paint. Of course, if someone saw them and wrote down the number, why would he throw it away?

The license plate number probably meant nothing. He knew that, but he decided to check it out anyway. In the past, his hunches had been right too often for him to ignore his instincts.

Maybe the paper had been dropped accidentally.

Officer Bremner hustled to his car and grabbed the phone. Within seconds the Motor Vehicle Department ran a computer check on the license plate number. The report came back: the owner of the car had a long history of traffic violations and had recently failed to appear in court on a drunk driving charge. There was a warrant out for his arrest.

The license plate number was quickly broadcast to every police unit in Oakwood.

Rosie lay in the dark, trying to figure out some way to help herself. She couldn't yell. She couldn't get untied. Maybe she could wriggle through the garbage until she was close enough to the side of the Dumpster that she could kick it and make some noise.

It was a long shot, she knew, but she had to try something. She couldn't just lie there in the garbage and hope that she would be discovered.

She bent her knees and tried to shove herself forward, but she did not move. She tried again but only succeeded in digging a small trench between her knees and her feet.

I'll have to roll over, she decided. The idea of lying facedown in the muck was not thrilling.

What if she flipped onto her stomach and got stuck that way?

She could think of no other way to get to the side of the Dumpster. She squeezed her eyes shut, in case garbage seeped in behind her glasses, and pressed her lips firmly against the bandanna. She wished she could hold her nose, as well.

She inhaled, held her breath, and turned, rolling easily onto her stomach. Something slimy squashed against her cheek. Quickly she rolled again, onto her back.

She could feel something caught in her hair, and whatever was on her cheek dripped down to her shoulder. She lifted her legs and kicked, moving her ankles back and forth. They found only air. She would have to roll again.

When she flipped facedown this time, she got cottage cheese up her nose. She raised her head and snorted, trying to blow the cottage cheese out before she rolled onto her back once more.

This time when she lifted her legs and kicked, the side of her foot hit the side of the Dumpster. She lay parallel to the front side of the Dumpster; she had to swing her feet sideways in order to make contact. She didn't have much force that way, and it hurt her ankle bone, but it did make some noise. If it was quiet on the playground, someone might hear her.

If someone was there to listen. It did no good to kick the Dumpster and make some noise when the school yard was empty.

Kayo, running hard, arrived back at doggie school after the class was dismissed.

"What's wrong with you?" asked Sammy. "You look like you just saw a monster movie."

"Something's happened to Rosie. I found her vocabulary notebook on the ground."

Sammy's mother stopped her car at the curb.

"She probably got tired of that dumb notebook and threw it away," Sammy said. He put Napoleon in the backseat and then got in the front with his mother.

The woman who had helped with registration said, "Are you Rosie Saunders?"

"I'm her friend. We came together."

"There was a phone call for Rosie. Her dad said to tell her that he had a flat tire and will be late picking her up."

Kayo bit her lip, wondering how long it took to change a tire. Should she wait for Mr. Saunders or should she try to reach Mrs. Saunders? Rosie

74

had said her mom went shopping, but she might be home by now. Kayo decided to call.

She got the Saunderses' answering machine. She did not leave a message. By the time Mrs. Saunders got it, Mr. Saunders would already be here.

All of the other people with dogs had gone home by then. Kayo and the registrar were the last to leave. The janitor locked the building and left.

"I'll wait with you," the registrar said, "but I hope he arrives soon. I have to get home before nine-thirty. My baby-sitter works nights and has to leave by nine-thirty."

"Mr. Saunders will be here any minute," Kayo said. "You don't need to stay with me."

"I can't leave you here alone."

Kayo didn't particularly want to stay there alone, but she didn't want to cause a problem for the registrar and the baby-sitter, either.

The registrar paced nervously back and forth on the sidewalk.

Kayo stood in the doggie school doorway and peered anxiously down the street, wondering what was taking Mr. Saunders so long. Didn't he know how to change a tire? Was he waiting for

AAA or a gas station to send someone to change it for him?

Kayo wondered if she should have called the police again and told them about the notebook. Well, it was too late now. The building was locked and the only telephone was inside.

If Mr. Saunders didn't get there soon, she would ask the registrar to drive her to the nearest supermarket or other place that had a public telephone. Her own mother would be home from choir practice by now; Mom would come and get her.

A white Camry approached.

"Here he comes," Kayo said. "Thanks for waiting."

"Thank goodness," said the registrar. She raced around the corner of the building to her own car.

Kayo stepped to the curb, but the white Camry continued past the dog school without stopping. The car looked exactly like Mr. Saunders's car. The driver was a stranger.

Kayo got to the corner of the building just in time to see the registrar's car pull out of the parking lot in the opposite direction.

Alone now, she returned to the doorway to wait.

Chapter

10

Jake Ignatio enjoyed working the night shift. There was less traffic at night, making it easier to maneuver the huge garbage truck. And the night shift picked up only from public buildings: shopping malls, schools, grocery stores, that kind of thing.

Jake used to work days, driving a regular garbage truck on a residential route. It had been interesting work. You could tell a lot about people from the contents of their garbage cans. Jake had never ceased to be amazed at the things people threw away. Perfectly good furniture, dishes, toys—you name it and Jake had seen it, in—or next to—somebody's garbage can. Once Jake found a practically new ten-speed bicycle propped against a can, with a note tied to the handlebars: *Garbage man—please take bike.*

That time Jake couldn't stand it. He took the bike, all right, but not to the dump. He took it to the closest Goodwill collection point and left it there.

At least on the night route he didn't cringe at that kind of waste as often. Most of the garbage he picked up from commercial buildings was just that: garbage.

He liked the night route for another reason, too. He worked alone, and as he drove, he listened to *Carmen* or *The Barber of Seville* or one of the other operas he loved, humming along with the music. Occasionally, unable to contain his enthusiasm, Jake burst into song himself.

Tonight he was listening to *Aida,* one of his favorites.

Jake turned into the service drive at George Washington Junior High School and headed toward the Dumpster. When he was almost there, he braked to a stop, leaving the headlights on.

He sat in the cab of the truck, with his Walkman earphones playing the Triumphal March from *Aida,* and stared. If that, thought Jake, doesn't beat all. Some nut has left a dog tied to

the Dumpster. I suppose they think I'll get rid of
it for them. Well, they can think again.

Jake climbed down from the cab of the truck
and approached the dog. The creature looked
scared and kept glancing at the enormous truck,
but it stood its ground, barking loudly as Jake
went closer.

"Calm down, dog," Jake muttered. "I won't
hurt you."

The dog seemed unconvinced. It barked again.

Inside the Dumpster, Rosie's pulse raced. She
heard Bone Breath's frantic barks and knew
someone was there. She raised her feet and
swung her ankle into the side of the Dumpster.
If it was the vandals returning, it didn't matter
if she made noise because they knew where she
was, anyway. If anyone else was out there, it was
crucial to make them hear her.

Thunk. Thunk. Thunk. Rosie kicked her feet
over and over again. Her shoe protected the side
of her foot, but her ankle bone throbbed from
being pounded against the hard metal. She knew
she was causing a major bruise, but she also
knew it was her one chance to be rescued.

Slowly Jake inched closer to the Dumpster, ex-
tending his fingers so the dog could smell them.
When he was about two feet away, the dog quit

barking. Jake had not heard the barking anyway, with the music blaring into both ears.

Jake took another step, still holding out his hand.

"Mmmmmm," said Rosie, making as much noise as it was possible to make with a bandanna stuffed in her mouth.

The dog sniffed Jake's fingertips and then licked Jake's hand. Jake smiled and unhooked the leash from the dog's collar, freeing the dog. Instead of running off, the dog stayed where it was, directly in front of the Dumpster.

"Scram," Jake said. "Get out of here, dog, so I can do my job."

The dog didn't move.

At the sound of a voice Rosie kicked even more frantically. Someone was out there. Whoever it was must hear her. Why didn't he respond?

Jake thought, The dog will move soon enough when I turn the truck back on. The noise of the grinders would send any sensible dog scampering away.

He climbed back into the truck, and the engine roared in the night. He drove past the side of the Dumpster and then shifted into reverse, easing the truck into position so he could lift the

Dumpster and dump the contents into the grinder.

Beep! Beep! Beep! The sound warned anyone behind the truck to get out of the way.

Beep! Beep! Beep!

Inside the Dumpster Rosie recognized the sound of the garbage truck and felt sick to her stomach.

It was here. Now. The worst possible nightmare she could imagine was about to come true, and there was nothing she could do to stop it.

In a panic Rosie raised her feet and banged her ankle against the side of the Dumpster, over and over, but even as she did it, she knew it was useless. No one would stand beside the Dumpster now, with the garbage truck approaching. And the truck made too much noise for anyone to hear Rosie unless they were next to the Dumpster.

Tears rolled down the sides of Rosie's face and pooled in her ears. A terrible, aching sadness overwhelmed her. She didn't want her life to end. Not yet! Not like this!

In the past, when Rosie argued with her parents, she sometimes daydreamed about how sorry they would be if she died. She imagined them weeping at her funeral and berating themselves for ever making Rosie unhappy.

Now, with the threat of death so real, she did not imagine her parents' grief. She focused on her own fear and rage and disappointment.

I want to live! Although she could not speak, the words poured forth from every cell in Rosie's body.

Thump! Thump! Her ankles clunked at the side of the Dumpster, and she forced continuous groans from her throat. She knew she couldn't be heard over the garbage truck's racket, but she was not willing to lie there in the stinking mess and not do anything to help herself. She had to keep trying.

Jake watched the dog in his rearview mirror. The creature had stationed itself directly in front of the Dumpster and stubbornly refused to move. As the truck came closer, the dog began to quiver with fear, but still it didn't budge. Jake had never seen anything like it. It was as if the dog was trying to protect the garbage Dumpster.

Jake flipped the control that turned on the grinders. They clanged and whirred into motion, creating additional noise, but still the little dog stayed in its chosen spot.

Jake knew he had two choices. One was to

keep backing until he was in place and then activate the lift that would go under the Dumpster to raise it up and dump its contents into the grinder. If he did that, the dog would almost surely be caught by the lift and either crushed against the Dumpster or lifted up and tossed into the grinder, along with the contents of the Dumpster. If he wanted to finish his route on schedule and get back to the garage in time to have coffee with the other drivers, that is what he should do. The other choice was to stop the truck and try to make the dog move out of the way.

The dog was a dang nuisance, but Jake had to admire its courage. He sighed and hit the brake. He'd probably get bit for his trouble, but he would give the dog one more chance.

Jake Ignatio approached the frightened dog again. As he grasped the dog's collar, headlights appeared behind him, lighting the Dumpster. Another vehicle drove slowly down the same service road that the garbage truck used.

Jake turned, wondering if this might be the dog's owner. The headlights of the garbage truck lit up the service road. Jake saw a white truck approach. There were small locked doors all along the sides of the truck; black letters proclaimed COUNTY ANIMAL CONTROL.

The dog catcher! Whoever had tied the dog to the Dumpster must also have called the dog catcher to come and get it. Jake's sense of fairness was outraged. What a cowardly way to get rid of such a brave little dog.

As he walked away from the Dumpster toward the Animal Control truck, he reached for the switch on his Walkman and turned off *Aida*. Verdi would roll in his grave, Jake thought, if he knew I stopped his music in the middle of an aria.

The Animal Control driver got out and nodded at Jake. "You the one who reported the stray?" he asked.

"No," said Jake.

"Well, somebody did. Took me awhile to get here, though."

"What happens to the dogs, after you take them?" Jake asked.

"They get forty-eight hours. If someone claims them before then, the owner pays a fine and takes the dog home."

"And if nobody claims them?"

The man shrugged. "Then it's all over. Have to make room for the next batch of strays."

"You do away with them even when they're young and healthy, like this one?"

"Hey! Don't tell *me* about it. My dog is fixed, you know what I mean? And he's kept in his own yard."

The man opened one of the doors on the side of the truck and removed a leash. He put gloves on—long gloves that protected his arms all the way to the elbows. Then he turned toward Bone Breath.

Bone Breath looked up at Jake. His tail hung limply between his legs, and his ears were so flat it looked as if he didn't have any.

Jake's heart went out to the miserable little dog. Poor thing. It deserved better than to be locked up for forty-eight hours and then . . .

"You can forget about taking this one," Jake said. His words surprised himself as much as they surprised the Animal Control man.

The man stopped walking and gave Jake a suspicious look. "It's your dog?" he said.

"It is now," Jake said.

The man cocked his head to one side. "You got a dog license?"

"I'll get one first thing tomorrow morning."

"Yeah? Well, don't let him run loose like this again."

"I won't," Jake said.

"Anyone who lets his dog run free should have my job for a week. You wouldn't believe how many dogs I shovel off the side of the street because they got hit by a car." The man removed his gloves and put them and the leash in the truck. "Have a good one," he said. He got in the truck and drove away.

Have a good what? Jake wondered. Good night? Good life? Good dog?

He looked at Bone Breath. What in heck am I going to do with a dog, he wondered. Especially one that thinks the garbage Dumpster is his mommy.

Jake turned his earphones back on. This was the most interrupted opera he'd ever listened to. He went back to the Dumpster and untied the leash. The dog walked to Jake and leaned against his leg, as if thanking him. Jake bent and picked him up. Beneath his fingers, he could feel the little dog's heart pounding with fear.

"You're going to be okay," Jake said. "You can stay with me until I find your owner."

He pulled some fur back from the dog's collar, to find where to attach the leash, and saw that someone had written the dog's name on the collar in indelible ink. Bone Breath. Jake chuckled. What a goofy name for a dog.

Bone Breath held still, snuggling into Jake's shoulder, as long as Jake stood beside the Dumpster. When Jake carried Bone Breath toward the garbage truck, to put him on the seat, Bone Breath struggled, fighting to get loose.

Jake tightened his grip, expecting at any second to feel teeth sink into his arm. Bone Breath kicked and twisted, but he did not bite. His breath came in short puffs; Jake decided the dog was aptly named.

Years of hoisting heavy garbage cans had given Jake bulging biceps. Even so, he barely managed to hang on to Bone Breath and get him in the truck.

"You don't make it easy to help you," he said as he got in, too, shut the door, and once again started backing toward the Dumpster.

Beep! Beep! Beep! The backup warning echoed across the playground.

Inside the Dumpster Rosie struggled to stand up. Since she couldn't make enough noise with her feet to attract attention, she had to try something else. If she could get to her feet, maybe she could jump high enough to push the lid of the

Dumpster open. Or at least make it clang and alert someone that she was inside.

It was not easy to stand up when she was lying flat with her hands tied behind her and her feet tied together. The harder Rosie tried, the deeper she sank in the mucky garbage.

The garbage truck quit *beeping*. Jake pushed the lever to activate the lift. He was anxious now to finish his route and get home. He wondered what his wife would say when she saw him bring a dog through the kitchen door. Jake smiled at the thought. Just this school Dumpster and one more, and then he'd be on his way home.

The metal claws of the lift eased under the Dumpster and clamped shut.

Chapter

11

Mr. Saunders finally arrived. Kayo saw the car approaching, but this time she waited until it stopped and she could see the driver before she ran to the curb.

"Where's Rosie?" Mr. Saunders asked. His face was smudged and his shirt was dirty.

Kayo quickly got in and told him everything that had happened—Bone Breath's escape, the vandals at George Washington Junior High, and Rosie's notebook on the playground.

When Kayo got to the part about the notebook, Mr. Saunders turned pale. "She's in trouble," he said. "She would never be careless with her vocabulary notebook."

As he drove toward the school, Mr. Saunders

called the police from his car phone. The police said they had not seen Rosie at George Washington Junior High.

"In that case," Mr. Saunders said, "I want to report a missing person."

The words brought tears to Kayo's eyes. She imagined Rosie's picture on the side of a milk carton. She thought of posters she had seen in store windows and tacked to telephone poles—posters showing people who had disappeared months earlier.

"She's twelve years old," Mr. Saunders said. "Brown hair, brown eyes, glasses. She may have her dog with her, a cairn terrier—he looks like Toto in *The Wizard of Oz* movie."

As Kayo listened to Mr. Saunders tell the police what Rosie was wearing, she wished with all her heart that she had never suggested taking Bone Breath to dog school. Their other Care Club project had been a disaster, too, but at least when the cat burglar caught them, she and Rosie were together. They had each other. This time Rosie faced an unknown danger alone, and Kayo felt completely helpless.

Maybe I should have stayed with Rosie, Kayo thought, instead of going to call the police. My call was not in time anyway.

No. If Rosie had been kidnapped by the vandals, as Kayo suspected, it would not help to have Kayo kidnapped, too. Still, it was awful to be left behind, waiting and wondering.

Not knowing. That was the worst part—not knowing where Rosie was.

As soon as Mr. Saunders finished talking to the police, he called Kayo's mom.

"Where are you?" Mrs. Benton cried when she heard his voice. "Where is Kayo?" Without waiting for him to answer, she said, "Someone called from the police station. They said Kayo saw vandals at George Washington School and called the police and I said Kayo wasn't at George Washington School, she was at dog obedience school, but when I tried to call there, nobody answered and I've been half out of my mind, wondering what is going on."

When Mrs. Benton paused for breath, Mr. Saunders apologized for not calling sooner. "I had a flat tire," he explained.

"Is Kayo all right? Do you know anything about any vandals?"

Mr. Saunders handed the telephone to Kayo.

"Hi, Mom," Kayo said. "I'm fine. I'll explain about the vandals when I get home." Kayo saw George Washington Junior High ahead. "I can't talk anymore," she said. "I have to help Mr. Saunders look for Rosie."

Mr. Saunders drove past the front of George Washington Junior High, turned the corner, and headed toward the parking lot beside the track.

"Look!" Kayo cried. "The garbage truck is here. It's going to empty the Dumpster that I tied Bone Breath to!"

Mr. Saunders slammed on the brakes and turned off the engine. Without bothering to take the key out of the ignition, he flung open the car door and bolted toward the garbage truck, waving his arms and shouting, "Wait! Wait! My dog is tied to the Dumpster."

Kayo jumped out and ran, too. "Stop!" she screamed.

Officer Bremner had just pulled wearily into the station lot when he heard the call. A missing child, a twelve-year-old girl. Last seen at George Washington Junior High about an hour ago. Possibly has a small dog with her. Toto lookalike.

Officer Bremner snapped to attention, every nerve on alert. Missing kids always got to him. He imagined how it would be if his Jessica disappeared, and the horror made it impossible for him to stay emotionally detached. This time it was more than just a missing girl; it was a dog, and a location Bremner had been to twice that night. An hour ago would be about the time the tip came in about the vandals.

Now that he thought about it, the little dog by the Dumpster did look like Toto. He ought to know; Jessica loved that movie.

Bremner wondered if Animal Control had been to the school yet. For the second time that night he drove out of the police station lot and headed back to George Washington Junior High.

If the dog was still there, he would pick it up and take it back to the station. One way or another he would wrestle it into his car, whether the dog wanted to go with him or not. Maybe he could wind the leash around the dog's jaw, like a muzzle, so it couldn't bite him.

He could justify the dog to the chief now; it was part of a missing person's case and not just a sad little stray.

Out of habit, Officer Bremner drove by Oakwood Elementary on his way to Elm Street. A lone car sat in the school's parking lot. He glanced at the license plate as he passed, and immediately hit the brake. The number matched the scrap of paper he'd found earlier.

Bremner's breath came faster and all thoughts

of a small dog flew out of his mind. He looked across the parking lot, beyond the portable classroom, toward the back wall of the school, where the second mural was. A shadow moved. Someone was there. He drove around the corner and parked.

He called in to say he was going to investigate suspicious activity behind Oakwood Elementary School. Then he climbed out of the patrol car and strode toward Oakwood's second mural.

I hope it's them, he thought. I hope I catch them with their stinking spray paint in their hands.

The phrase *red-handed* popped into Officer Bremner's mind and he shook his head at the irony. If he wasn't so angry, it would be funny.

Rosie wished she could cover her ears, to blot out the clang and whir of the garbage truck's machinery. The noise surrounded her, loud and menacing. At any moment she expected the Dumpster to move, as it was lifted in the air above the truck. How long did she have after the Dumpster started to move? Ten seconds? Thirty?

She lay on her side, bent her knees, and raised her shoulders. She was able to get on her knees, but she couldn't get her feet under her enough to stand up.

Clunk! Something metal banged the bottom of the Dumpster, jolting it up about an inch.

Half a minute to live. The thought sent new strength and determination. Rosie sat up and extended her legs in front of her. Then she bent her knees and rocked back and forth, rocking harder and harder to build some momentum until she was able to lift herself to a squatting position. From there, at last, she made it to her feet.

Garbage covered her shoes and oozed toward the bottom of her jeans, but she didn't care. She was upright.

The Dumpster jerked again. Rosie swayed. With her feet together and her hands tied, she was unable to keep her balance, and she fell face first into the trash.

She knew what caused the jolts. The metal lift was now in place, and any second the Dumpster would rise into the air and be turned upside down, its contents spilled into the steel jaws of the grinders.

With the lift in place under the Dumpster, Jake Ignatio reached for the lever again, this time to shift it into the Up position. As his fingers touched the lever, the little dog beside him began to yap and jump with excitement. Jake leaned forward to see what the dog was so worked up about and saw a man and a girl running toward him, waving their hands.

Now what? thought Jake. At this rate I'll never finish my route tonight. Or *Aida*, either. He clicked off the music and, leaving the truck running, got out to see what the man and the girl wanted.

Sweat trickled down Rosie's neck as she struggled to stand up again. This time, after she was in a sitting position, she scooted across the garbage until her shoulder bumped the wall. It would be easier to steady herself if she had something to lean against. Once more she bent her legs, rocked to a squatting position, and made it to her feet.

She expected the Dumpster to lurch again. Whenever she had watched the garbage truck in action, the lift went under the Dumpster, clamped it tight, and immediately raised the Dumpster and emptied it, all in less than a minute. She still heard the noise of the engine and the grinder, but the Dumpster did not move.

Leaning against the wall, Rosie crouched and jumped straight up. Bonk! Her head struck the metal roof. It felt like someone had banged her on the head with a hammer. Tears sprang to her eyes, and she leaned dizzily into the wall, waiting for the pain to subside.

Mr. Saunders shouted over the noise of the truck, "Have you seen a little girl? And a dog?"

"There was a dog tied to the Dumpster," Jake yelled. "It's in my truck."

Kayo rushed to look in the window. "That's him!" she cried. "It's Bone Breath."

"I figured somebody was trying to get rid of him," Jake said.

"What about a girl?" Mr. Saunders said. He pointed at Kayo. "The same age as this girl."

Jake shook his head. "Haven't seen any kids tonight," he said. He opened the door of the truck. Bone Breath went crazy when Mr. Saunders picked him up and put him on the ground. He ran in circles, yipping and yelping.

"Here's his leash," Jake said, handing it to Kayo. "Don't ever tie your dog to a Dumpster again; he's lucky to be alive."

"It's a long story," Mr. Saunders said, "and I have to get down to the police station. Thanks for rescuing Bone Breath."

"Glad to be of help," Jake said. He climbed back in the truck and turned on the grinders.

97

When Mr. Saunders bent to snap the leash on Bone Breath's collar, Bone Breath bolted away. He ran directly to the Dumpster and plopped down in front of it.

"Bone Breath!" called Mr. Saunders. "Come here!"

Bone Breath ignored him.

Jake called out the window of the truck, "He's done that all night. He acts like he's guarding the Dumpster."

"I think he's scared of the truck," Mr. Saunders said. "Would you mind turning it off, just long enough for me to carry him away?"

Jake switched off the grinders. He pushed the lever to stop the lift. He turned off the engine. One by one, every piece of machinery stopped.

The sudden silence made every nerve in Rosie's body more alert. First the lift didn't move right away and now the grinders stopped. Then the truck stopped, too. What was going on out there?

"Thanks!" called Mr. Saunders. "It'll just take me a minute."

Dad? Rosie's heart thumped in her throat. Dad was out there, talking to someone.

Rosie bent her knees and prepared to jump again. She hoped she wouldn't hurt herself, banging her head on the metal roof this way, but anything was better than being chopped up by the garbage grinders.

Mr. Saunders marched over to the Dumpster and picked up Bone Breath. Bone Breath struggled and tried to get away.

"Fool dog," Mr. Saunders muttered. "We don't have time for this now." He turned away from the Dumpster and started back to his car, with Bone Breath struggling to jump out of his arms. Kayo ran alongside Mr. Saunders, trying to keep Bone Breath from getting away.

"Mnmmmph," said Rosie.

Kayo looked back. What was that? She thought she had heard someone moan, but when she looked she saw only the big green Dumpster and the garbage truck. Kayo turned her attention back to Bone Breath.

Rosie gathered every bit of energy she had left and jumped, springing up out of the garbage. *Clang!* Her head struck the roof again, causing it to reverberate.

Kayo stopped. What was that noise? It sounded like someone banging on the Dumpster. She looked at the truck. The driver was climbing back in. Mr. Saunders, clinging to Bone Breath, was nearly to the car. There was no one else here. What had she heard?

Rosie's head throbbed as she prepared to jump again. If I have to die, Rosie decided, I'll die trying to save myself.

Jake Ignatio put the headset on and pressed the button to start Act Four of *Aida*. Then he started the truck's engine and turned on the grinders again.

Frantically trying to keep her balance, Rosie clenched her teeth against the pain in her head and made one last leap.

Desperation gave strength to her weary leg muscles. She leaped higher this time, and hit harder.

Her head forced the Dumpster lid six inches up. Blood trickled down Rosie's forehead as she slumped forward, still as stone, on top of the garbage.

Blackness surrounded her.

The lid clanged back down with a loud *THUNK*, but Rosie did not hear it.

Chapter

12

Officer Bremner stayed close to the side of Oakwood Elementary School, his hand poised over his holster. His mouth was dry and every nerve in his body seemed stretched like a tightrope. Ahead, he heard laughter.

He listened to their talk, sorting out the voices. There were three of them. Good. The report from George Washington School had said three, and Bremner wanted all of them.

He eased forward, watching, as the men removed tops from cans of spray paint and aimed them toward Oakwood Elementary's second mural.

Officer Bremner waited. If he nabbed them now, some sharp defense lawyer would get them off on circumstantial evidence, claiming they never intended to paint the mural. Bremner wanted to time it exactly right. He would make the arrest after they started painting but before they did much damage.

"We'll teach 'em," one of the men said. "They can't expel my brother and get away with it."

"We're fixing 'em," another man said.

Officer Bremner frowned. Was that the motive for all this destruction? Revenge because some hoodlum kid got kicked out of school?

Zzt. Zzt. Zzt. Three paint cans sprayed in unison.

"Drop the paint and put your hands in the air," Officer Bremner said. It gave him great satisfaction to see the men comply.

Kayo rushed to the Dumpster and pounded on the back side. "Hello!" she called. "Is someone in there?"

There was no answer.

She couldn't open the lid to look in, because the hinge was in back. The truck was flush against the front side of the Dumpster, with the lift mechanism going between the two. There wasn't room for Rosie to get between the garbage truck and the Dumpster, and, even if there had been, she would have been afraid of being crushed.

"Mr. Saunders!" Kayo cried. "I heard a noise from inside the Dumpster!"

Mr. Saunders, with his attention on Bone Breath, did not hear Kayo over the racket of the garbage truck. It was all he could do to hang on to the still-struggling Bone Breath while he opened the back door of the car. The fool dog acted as if Mr. Saunders was trying to murder him. If one night at obedience school made him this frantic, perhaps Rosie should drop out.

Rosie. Where was Rosie? Fear for his daughter's safety washed over Mr. Saunders as he managed to deposit Bone Breath on the backseat. He slammed the door shut before Bone Breath could jump out.

As he opened the front door, he realized Kayo was no longer beside him. Looking back, he saw that she was still over by the Dumpster. What was wrong with that girl? Surely she must realize they needed to get to the police station. The cops would want a picture of Rosie.

"Kayo!" he called. "Let's go!"

Kayo pounded once more on the back of the Dumpster, but there was no response. Had she imagined she heard something inside? Had it only been another noise from the truck?

No. The first noise came before the truck was turned back on. She was sure of it.

"Mr. Saunders!" Kayo shouted. "I think there might be someone in the Dumpster. Someone alive!"

Muttering to himself, Mr. Saunders hurried to see what Kayo was yelling about this time.

Inside the truck Jake shifted the lever to start the lift. The lift jerked into motion, slowly hoisting the Dumpster into the air.

When Kayo saw the Dumpster begin to rise, she didn't wait for Mr. Saunders. She raced straight toward the truck.

"Stop!" she shouted. "There's someone in the Dumpster!"

Jake leaned his head against the back of the seat, letting the music engulf him. In his mind he saw the pageantry of ancient Egypt. He saw Aida, hiding in the tomb to share her lover's tragic fate.

The Dumpster moved upward. It was three feet off the ground now.

Four feet.

Five.

Rosie lay unmoving and unaware.

Kayo pounded on the door of the truck, on the other side from the driver. Screaming at the driver to stop the engine, she looked through the window and realized the driver wore a headset, probably to block out the noise of the grinders. His eyes were closed. Reaching up, she yanked on the door handle. The door was locked.

The lift raised the Dumpster higher, paused momentarily, and then eased inward, toward the opening on top of the truck.

Rosie raced around the front of the truck to the driver's side, stepped up on the bumper, yanked on the door handle, and opened the door.

Startled, Jake jumped and glared at her.

The lift tilted. The Dumpster lid opened. The grinders roared.

"Stop it!" Kayo screamed. "Please! Make it stop!" Tears streamed down her cheeks as she looked back and up toward the Dumpster.

Jake couldn't hear the girl's words, but he saw sheer panic on her face. He reached forward and shifted the lever, stopping the lift. He halted the grinders, turned the truck's ignition key off, and, reluctantly, stopped his music.

The Dumpster dangled over the grinders, swaying slightly.

Mr. Saunders rushed to the truck and stood behind Kayo.

"I heard noise inside the Dumpster!" Kayo cried.

"What kind of noise?" Jake asked.

"It sounded as if someone was in there."

"Rosie!" said Mr. Saunders.

The color drained out of Jake Ignatio's face.

"My daughter is missing," Mr. Saunders said. "The police are looking for her, and she was last seen at this school."

Jake wiped perspiration from his brow. *Aida* seemed unimportant.

"The noise was a bang," Kayo said, "like someone pounding on the side."

"Rosie was here at the school earlier tonight," Mr. Saunders said, "looking for her dog."

"The dog I found," said Jake. His hand shook as he started the engine and reversed the lift.

Kayo and Mr. Saunders watched as the Dumpster jerked slowly downward. When it was back on the ground, Jake turned everything off and climbed out of the truck. Mr. Saunders and Kayo stood at one end of the Dumpster. Jake stepped onto the lift, grasped the lid on the front of the Dumpster, and opened it. Together, they looked inside.

Rosie, her eyes closed, lay on the pile of garbage. Blood dripped from a gash on her head.

Chapter

13

Rosie was released from the hospital the next morning. That afternoon Kayo bought a book that she knew Rosie wanted to read, gift-wrapped it, and took it to Rosie's house.

"She's in bed," Mrs. Saunders told Kayo, "but you can visit her for a little while."

"How is she?"

"Much better. Her ankle is badly bruised and she still has a headache, but that's to be expected with a concussion."

The sweet smell of cinnamon rolls baking filled the Saunderses' house. Kayo knew home-made cinnamon rolls were Rosie's favorite treat.

Mrs. Saunders handed Kayo a red envelope.

"You can take this to her," she said. "Someone dropped it off earlier, when Rosie was asleep. I forgot about it until you knocked."

Kayo climbed the stairs to Rosie's room. Rosie lay with her head propped on two pillows. Her black cat, Webster, was curled in a ball beside her.

"You look a lot better than you did the last time I saw you," Kayo said.

Rosie petted Webster. "I never want to see the inside of a garbage can again," she said.

"You smell better, too," Kayo said.

"Thanks. The nurses didn't want to let me shampoo my hair yet, but I couldn't stand it."

Kayo pulled Rosie's desk chair over to the bed and sat down. "I'm glad you're okay," she said. "I was so scared when I found your notebook."

"Not half as scared as I was."

"Did you see the article in the *Daily Herald?*"

"No. I didn't get home from the hospital until almost noon, and I went right to sleep after I got here."

Kayo took the newspaper clipping out of her tote bag and handed it to Rosie.

"Will you read it to me, please?" Rosie said.

"My head still hurts, and I don't want to put my glasses on."

Kayo read the article aloud.

DOG HERO SAVES OWNER;
VANDALS CAUGHT

A small dog named Bone Breath saved the life of his twelve-year-old mistress Friday night after the girl was tied up, gagged, and left in the Dumpster behind George Washington Junior High School.

When the county garbage truck arrived to empty the Dumpster, the dog refused to move out of the way. Truck driver Jake Ignatio told police, "That dog deserves a medal for bravery. When I backed my truck up close, he was so scared he was shaking, but he stayed next to the Dumpster, guarding it. If he had moved, the girl would be dead. The dog risked his own life to save the girl."

The girl was put in the Dumpster by three men after she discovered them painting the statue in front of the school. The men were later arrested at Oakwood Elementary School when Officer Ken Bremner caught them spray-

109

ing yellow paint on a mural. Bremner was praised by Chief Brian Stravinski for his alertness in spotting a car belonging to one of the suspects. Fingerprints found on empty paint cans at other vandalized schools matched those of the suspects.

When questioned about their motive for the two-week vandalism spree, the three men refused to answer. School officials confirmed that the younger brother of one of the men was permanently expelled from the Oakwood School District on the day that the first episode of vandalism occurred. All three men are being held without bail.

"It doesn't mention our names," Kayo complained. "You would think after I called to report the vandals and you nearly got killed that we'd get some credit."

"Mom told them not to," Rosie said. "There was a reporter at the hospital, and I heard Mom ask him not to use either of our names in the paper. She was afraid the vandals or some of their buddies would try to get back at us for turning them in."

"Oh." Kayo handed Rosie the red envelope.

"This is for you," she said. "Your mom said some-body brought it over. I suppose it's a get-well card."

"Will you read that to me, too?"

Kayo tore open the envelope and removed a piece of yellow tablet paper. "It's a get-well poem," she said. "From Sammy Hulenback."

"Get-well messages are supposed to cheer me up, not make me sicker."

Kayo grinned. "You made me listen when he wrote that awful poem to me."

"Oh, all right. What does it say?"

Kayo began.

>*"I'm glad that you*
>*Weren't chopped in two."*

Rosie groaned.

"There's another verse," Kayo said.

"I hope it's better than the first one."

Kayo kept reading:

>*"Do not worry; do not fear,*
>*You'll only stink for about a year."*

Kayo collapsed in a fit of giggles.

"That is the worst poem I ever heard," said Rosie. "What a wallydraigle!"

When Kayo caught her breath she said, "Wally-draigle: a feeble, imperfectly developed, and slovenly creature."

Rosie blinked in surprise. "You remembered," she said.

"I looked it up this morning," Kayo admitted. "I thought it might make you feel better if I used this week's vocabulary word."

"Thanks," Rosie said. "Would you please make a check mark in my notebook for me?"

"Where is it?"

Rosie reached in her pajama pocket.

"I might have known," said Kayo.

Mrs. Saunders came in carrying two plates, each containing a cinnamon roll. Bone Breath trotted beside her, hoping she might drop them.

"Bone Breath's dog school instructor called," Mrs. Saunders said. "She saw his name in the paper. She asked if you will be in class next Friday because she wants to give Bone Breath an award for bravery."

"We'll be there," said Rosie.

"It's an official Care Club project," said Kayo.

Mrs. Saunders said, "Have you noticed that whenever you girls have a Care Club project you end up in trouble?"

"Coincidence," said Rosie.

"Pure coincidence," said Kayo.

As soon as Mrs. Saunders left, Rosie gave Bone Breath a piece of her cinnamon roll. Bone Breath swallowed it without chewing. "Bone Breath deserves an award for bravery," she said.

"On Friday," Kayo said, "let's tell Sammy he was right. Dogs *do* resemble their owners."

About the Author

Peg Kehret's popular novels for young readers are regularly nominated for state awards. She has received the Young Hoosier Award, the Golden Sower Award, the Iowa Children's Choice Award, the Celebrate Literacy Award, and the Pacific Northwest Writers Conference Achievement Award. She lives with her husband, Carl, and their animal friends in Washington State, where she is a volunteer at the Humane Society and SPCA. Her two grown children and four grandchildren live in Washington, too.

Peg's Minstrel titles include *Nightmare Mountain; Sisters, Long Ago; Cages; Terror at the Zoo; Horror at the Haunted House;* and the *Frightmares*™ series.

Don't miss any of the adventure!

FRIGHTMARES™

Whenever pets–and their owners–get into trouble, Rosie Saunders
and Kayo Benton always seem to be in the middle of the action.
Ever since they started the Care Club ("We Care About Animals"),
they've discovered a world of mysteries and surprises. . .and danger!

CAT BURGLAR ON THE PROWL

BONE BREATH AND THE VANDALS

DON'T GO NEAR MRS. TALLIE
(coming in mid-July 1995)

By Peg Kehret

A MINSTREL® BOOK

Published by Pocket Books

1049-01

Award-winning author
Patricia Hermes brings you:

THE COUSINS' CLUB SERIES

#1: I'LL PULVERIZE YOU, WILLIAM
87966-9/$3.50

Summer will never be the same for the Cousins' Club
. . . both creepy cousin William and an out-of-control
boa constrictor have slithered into their vacation
plans!

#2: EVERYTHING STINKS
87967-7/$3.50

Just one perfect day of fun–that's all that everyone in
the Cousins' Club wants. But then one incredible
event changes their very idea of perfect. . . .

Watch for #3:
THIRTEEN THINGS NOT TO
TELL A PARENT
coming in the fall of 1995!

 A MINSTREL BOOK

Published by Pocket Books

1039-01

The Midnight Society has a scary
new story to tell. . .

A brand new thriller series based on the hit
Nickelodeon® show!

THE TALE OF THE
SINISTER STATUES

by **John Peel**

A new title every other month!!

A MINSTREL® BOOK

Published by Pocket Books

1053-01